CLIFFHANGER

SKIP PRESS

Artesian Press
P.O. Box 355, Buena Park, CA 90621

Take Ten Books
Adventure

Other Take Ten Themes:

Mystery
Sports
Disaster
Chillers
Thrillers
Fantasy
Horror
Romance

Project Editor: Liz Parker
Illustrator: Fujiko
Cover Designer: Tony Amaro
©2000 Artesian Press

All rights reserved. No part of this publication may be reproduced or transmitted in any form without permission in writing from the publisher. Reproduction of any part of this book, through photocopy, recording, or any electronic or mechanical retrieval system, without the written permission of the publisher, is an infringement of copyright law.

www.artesianpress.com

Artesian **Press**   ISBN 1-58659-011-1

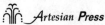

400660141

CONTENTS

Chapter 1

"A bloodthirsty soldier of fortune he was!" Hiro Yakamura read aloud, almost shouting, as he waited on the cliffside. "Redbeard was the terror of the Spanish main, a killer with a heart of steel, and now he had Lucinda in his grasp." He paused, looking over the words he had written. "Yeah," he said softly to himself. "End of chapter." Then, much louder--

"How did you like it, Jake?"

"Great!" came a voice from below. "Comin' up!"

A rope tied to the old pine tree nearby shook. Hiro put down his notebook and pen and grabbed a handhold on the rope. He peered over the edge of the cliff just in time to see Jake Adams climb to the top. He jumped out of the way as his blond-headed friend made it up the rope, breathing hard.

"Wow!" Hiro exclaimed. "That was *fast*!"

"How fast?" Jake asked, leaning up against the trunk of the ancient pine, catching his breath. Jake looked over at the notebook. "Writing another 'cliffhanger,' huh?"

Hiro didn't answer. He felt embarrassed. A cliffhanger was a story where the main character was always getting out of trouble, one scene to the next.

Hiro looked around frantically. Talk about trouble. He'd blown it! Of all the days to forget to wear his watch. . .

"Look in your pocket, Hiro," said Jake. "You put my stopwatch in there, so you wouldn't lose it. Remember?"

Hiro reached into his pants pocket. Sure enough, he pulled out the stopwatch and offered an embarrassed grin. "Sorry?"

"Sorry is right," Jake replied, gathering up his mountaineering gear and pulling in his rope. He tossed his second line over one shoulder as he frowned at Hiro. "How am I going to know how I'm doing, if you can't keep the stopwatch?"

Hiro lowered his head, not knowing what to say. He was still fairly new to America, and very new to the community where they both lived. Jake was a loner, but for some reason he had become his friend. Jake even liked the stories that Hiro spent time writing to practice his English. Plus, Jake's reactions helped to make the stories better. Now he had failed Jake--and it wasn't the first time. He just got so caught up in writing the stories. . .

"I am very sorry," Hiro said, unable to look at Jake. "Next time, I will leave my writing at home."

Jake chuckled and socked Hiro playfully on the arm.

"Forget it. Just leave the stopwatch out where you can see it next time, okay? I time myself for a reason."

As they walked back along the cliffs, they took turns tossing rocks into the sea far below. Jake always threw them much farther. He was a dedicated athlete who wanted to be a mountain climber. Hiro admired him greatly.

Hiro crinkled an eyebrow. "Hey, Jake, you know what 'soldier of fortune' means?"

Jake thought about it. "That's like our dads, right?" He looked hopefully at his new Japanese friend. "You know, they go out and fight to make money."

"Well . . ." Hiro replied. Then, after thinking it over--"Maybe I'll just say *pirates*."

"Oh, right," Jake said, faking it. "Yeah, that's better."

"*Hai*," Hiro replied--"yes" in

Japanese. He watched Jake tossing rocks, wishing he were as brave and athletic as his larger, older friend. It was almost night, and the cliffs of Portuguese Bend were bathed in the beautiful, dark red rays of sunset that had been common lately.

"Hey, Jake, know whey the sunsets are so red lately? I read in *Science Digest* it's because of the extra dust in the air from the eruption of the Mount Pinatubo volcano in the Philippines. Do you ever read *Science Digest*?"

Jake didn't answer. Hiro had noticed that Jake never talked much about his own reading or studying. "I'm going back," Jake said suddenly, turning on his heel.

"But it's late," Hiro protested. "It'll be dark soon."

"Go home if you want to," Jake said, walking past. "That climb was really slow. I can do better."

Hiro considered the situation, but

not for long. He caught up to Jake and took the stopwatch back. Jake pointed out how the dial glowed in the dark. Hiro took his usual position as Jake began backing down the cliff, bouncing off the wall at ten foot intervals, sliding down the rope like a pro. Pretty soon he called out—he was at the bottom. Then the rope went tight. Jake was making another climb.

It was really dark now. There were no street lights in their small community, and the houses were high above them, at least half a mile off. Out across the ocean, Hiro could see the lights of Sunset Beach, where he used to live. He found himself wondering if anyone cared about pirate stories anyway.

His thoughts were soon broken, however, when he heard a scramble of dirt and falling rocks below him, followed by a yell! Then silence, which was even scarier. Hiro scrambled to the edge of the cliff and looked down. His

heart jumped into his throat. There was
Jake, hanging by one leg, his body
scraping against the cliff. Hiro could
barely make out the outlines of the cliff,
but it looked like a section had broken

off just as Jake stepped on it.

"Jake!" Hiro screamed. No reply. Hiro felt his throat go dry. What should he do?

He looked back up toward the houses of Portuguese Bend. It was a long way up the hill, and if he went for help, what might happen to Jake? Would he slip out of the rope and fall? Hiro's house was closest to the cliffs, but there were no lights on.

Then he remembered his parents had gone to an early dinner. Business. He looked over the cliff again, trying to force himself to stop shaking. Thankfully, Jake's rope was still tight. Then he heard more falling rocks and dirt below and took another look. He had to act quickly. A solution came to him--there by the tree was Jake's extra line.

Moving quickly, Hiro fastened the rope as securely as possible to the old pine tree. He tried to remember the handholds Jake had taught him, and the special around-the-elbow loop for lowering yourself down. It worked! Hiro gulped, then took a deep breath. He turned his back to the cliff and started over, making sure he did nothing to bump Jake's rope. The crazy thing was, this was no story. This was a real "cliffhanger." Hiro had to get it perfect the first time. The life of his friend--his only friend--depended on it!

Chapter 2

Hiro took one step over the cliff, and made the mistake of looking down. It was a hundred feet of more down to the sea, and the rocky beach. Sure, the cliffs sloped down, but at a very steep angle. If you fell, it might be your last fall. And what if he hit Jake on the way down? Then they would both be killed. Hiro stepped back to the top, and started running.

There was a trail nearby, which cut down the cliff sideways. Surfers used it almost every day to get down to the beach. Hiro hustled down the path, watching his step. As he eased through a wedge in the rock cliff face, he saw that the sun was almost down. He hurried. A couple of times the loose soil and gravel slipped from beneath his feet, but the going was a lot easier than climbing down a rope. Hiro choked back the dust he stirred up, praying that Jake would be all right.

Hiro made it to the bottom of the trail and took off running along the rocks of the beach. He could see Jake hanging there, still unmoving, maybe fifty feet off the ground.

"Jake!" he yelled as he got to the rocks at the bottom of the cliff. "Jake, can you hear me?!"

No answer. Hiro caught his breath and grabbed the second rope he had thrown down. Now he had to climb up. Would it have been easier, letting himself down? No, he wasn't that strong. But what would he do once he made it to Jake?

There was no time to think. Hiro began to climb, remembering what Jake had told him--breathe out when you climb, breathe in when you rest, find firm footholds, then use them for leverage. There was a science to mountaineering, that was for sure, but Hiro didn't know it very well. Still, he

didn't seem to be straining. "Adrenalin," he told himself. The adrenalin in his body was pumped up, giving him extra strength in a tough situation.

"Jake!" Hiro cried, securing the rope around his elbow as he made it to where Jake was hanging. Still no answer. At least Jake was still breathing, but barely. There was a patch of blood midway up one pant leg. He reached out lightly, trying to wake up his friend, but it didn't work. Then Hiro slipped on the rope, dropping down several feet before he could catch himself!

"Yaggghhh!" he yelled, screaming at the pain in his hands. Rope burn! Jake had warned him about it a dozen times. Hiro gritted his teeth, then looked down. The rocks below looked menacing, colored red by the sunset. It reminded Hiro of blood. Real blood . Jake's blood. *His* blood. He gritted his teeth and started pulling himself back toward Jake.

He was beginning to wonder if either one of them would make it through this, but he shook the thought out of his head. This was no time to be troubled with worry. Hiro looped the rope around his waist and elbow, and tied a half-hitch Jake had taught him. He was amazed that he tied the knot correctly. With one arm free, he grabbed the slack from Jake's rope and tied his friend up more securely. Then he realized that the blood racing to Jake's head was dangerous. He had to get him in an upright position. Hiro braced himself against the cliff and began using his shoulder. It was a tremendous struggle, and when he happened to glance at the rocks below, he felt like he would pass out. But finally he managed to get Jake upright and tie him there securely.

The adrenalin was spent now. Hiro

was exhausted as he tied the final knot in Jake's line. That was all he could do. Jake was too heavy for anything else. It would be impossible for Hiro to pull Jake up from on top of the cliff, or even lower him down slowly using the tree for leverage. He needed to get help, period.

"I gotta get some more people, Jake," Hiro said, trying to sound as comforting and calm as possible. "Listen, I know unconscious people can hear things around them sometimes. You're gonna be all right, okay? Just. . ." Hiro shook his head and groaned. He almost said "hang in there."

"Just don't worry, Jake," he continued. "I'll be back soon. You'll be all right."

Jake still hadn't stirred, which worried Hiro even more. But he had to take action. He began lowering himself down. Suddenly, he slipped on the rope, and fell the last five feet. He lay still on the bushes he had landed on, mentally feeling his body. Nothing felt broken or terribly bruised, but he realized just how tired he had become. Pulling himself to a sitting position, he looked up at Jake. The knots seemed to be holding just fine. Hiro just had to get someone strong enough to pull Jake up.

Then he heard something that scared him to death. Thunder! He jerked his head toward the horizon. Looking in the sky, he saw lightening and rain clouds moving in off the sea.

Chapter 3

Gathering his strength, Hiro got to his feet. Ow! His right foot felt like someone had hit it with a hammer. He lifted his foot and examined it. There it was. The swelling had already started. He had twisted his ankle badly. Great! Now what?

As he glanced back up at Jake, drops of liquid hit his face. Oh, no. Blood?! Hiro wiped his face with his hand, then looked back up. He could see it now, dropping down in the scarce light. Rain. Of all times for a storm!

A thought seemed to come from nowhere. Hiro remembered a conversation he had with his grandfather, who sometimes cut himself when gardening. Any pain could be dealt with, Grandfather said. You simply refused to agree that it could stop you. "If you confront a tiger face to face," Grandfather had said, "the tiger will hesitate. He may still bite you, but he will hesitate."

Hiro laughed to himself. The pain was still there, but he could fight it off. He had to, and there was no time to waste. Favoring his injured ankle slightly, he hurried to the steep cliff trail and began to climb. The rain was coming down steadily now. Not a downpour, but steady. It pelted into the loose dust of the trail, making little splattering sounds as it hit. It wasn't hard climbing, except for his ankle. Everytime he felt some pain, though, he thought about his grandfather's joke and chuckled a little. It made the tiger hesitate.

Now a tiny stream of water was

coming down the tail , run-off from the rain. Hiro found himself slipping and sliding on the mud, and more than once he banged his body against the rocky cliff. His handholds were desperate but sure, and he felt more confident the farther he climbed up the cliff. Tired and choking for breath, he forced himself to continue by sheer will alone. Finally, he was almost there. He scrambled with his feet and hands toward the top of the trail. Then lightning crackled, and a loud boom of thunder shook the sky! Startled, Hiro lost his footing and found himself sliding down the trail!

Luckily, he slid sideways into the part of the trail that cut through a narrow wedge of rock. It stopped his slide. Again, he ran a mental check of his body. He was scratched and bruised, but again it seemed like nothing was broken. Hiro got to his feet and continued faster than before, with strength he didn't know he had. Before he knew it, he was lying on top of the cliff, face first, gasping for breath.

Hiro raised his head and looked around. The ropes! The thought seemed to wake him up and give him more strength. Half-crawling, he made it to where the ropes were tied to the old pine tree. Hiro tested them. They were still as tight as before. The rain was steady now, though, and Hiro saw water runoff going down the cliff, right below the ropes. Wincing against his pain, he struggled to his feet. Holding on to the secondary rope for security, he eased toward the edge of the cliff.

"Hiro," came a weak voice. "Help me." Jake!

Chapter 4

Jake was moving, ever so slightly. The water was running down the cliff, splashing here and there, and rain was hitting the side of the cliff as well. Little bits of mud slid down the cliffside and occasional small rocks came loose and fell.

"Jake!" Hiro yelled. "You're conscious!"

"Of course I'm conscious!" Jake yelled back, choking and coughing. "Why am I tied up like this?"

"'Cause you fell!" Hiro shouted. "I had to tie you there. You were hanging upside down like a bat!"

Some mud and rocks fell toward Jake. He ducked his head and moved his body to swing out of the way. In doing so, he slammed against the cliff wall.

"Yagghhhh!" Jake screamed. "That hurts!"

Hiro wiped the rain off his face and squinted his eyes. Jake was holding his leg, in the place on his pants where Hiro had seen the blood.

"Are you all right, Jake?"

"My leg hurts a lot!" Jake moaned again and braced himself for the cliff. He was silent for a few moments. "Go get a doctor," he said finally. "There's a doctor in the village."

"Huh? What village, Jake?"

Jake didn't answer. He was singing to himself now. "*Three blind mice, see how they run. Three blind mice, see how they run.*" Singing, and laughing.

Hiro stood up, shaking his head. He had read about this. Jake was getting delirious. "Exposure," they called it. Probably the fall and the exposure were making Jake lose his senses.

Hiro looked back toward the houses above them. It was a mile or more back to where they lived, and there were no street lights in the community. It was raining all over the peninsula. Lightning cracked and thunder roared down from the hills. Suddenly, the lights in a section of houses went dark. The lightning had knocked out the electricity. If he ran across the open field between the cliffs and the houses, he would be at the highest point in the field--a perfect target for lightning. Should he risk it or try to pull Jake up?

Hiro felt himself starting to panic. He held the rope and leaned over to talk to Jake.

"Jake! This lightning is bad. You gotta pull yourself up, man. I'll help you. Use the leg that's not hurt. You gotta try it, Jake!"

Jake was still singing. *"They all went after the farmer's wife. She cut off their tails with a carving knife. Have you ever seen such a sight in your life? Three blind mice."*

Hiro sat back against the tree, feeling a great deal of grief and hopelessness. Then he willed himself out of the grief and got angry. He braced himself against a root of the pine tree and started trying to pull Jake up. At least Jake stopped singing the song. And he was doing it! He was actually pulling Jake up!

That didn't last long. The rope burns on his hands stung terribly and Hiro just wasn't strong enough. He had to lower Jake down again. Hiro looked over the side. Jake was still awake, and babbling something about climbing Mount Everest. And now Hiro started feeling the pain in his ankle. The tiger was biting, he told himself. He had to do something.

"If you don't pull yourself together, mate, I'll hang you me self!" Hiro roared. "I'm Redbeard the Pirate, meanest man on the Seven Seas!"

Jake stopped babbling and looked up toward Hiro. "Who is that? Who's up there?"

It worked! Hiro pressed the attack. "It's Redbeard!" he yelled. "If you don't get it together down there, I'll cut the line and send you tumbling to the ocean, har har!"

Jake kept staring at him, then looked down and out to sea. He seemed confused. Hiro gritted his teeth. What if he'd only confused Jake? What if he made Jake worse, or frantic? He could pull himself loose and fall to his death.

"Jake, listen! I . . ."

"It is you!" Jake yelled. "Hiro, what's the matter with you?! I'm hanging here freezing to death and you're acting like a pirate. Get me off this cliff, man!"

Hiro breathed a sigh of relief. Just a

crazy, wild idea, but it worked. He pulled out a stopwatch and showed it to Jake.

"Look, Jake, I've got the stopwatch. I'll time you getting yourself back up the cliff. You gotta help me, okay?"

"Okay, but my leg hurts, Hiro, bad!"

"You gotta try, Jake. Maybe we can do it together!"

"Okay, okay."

Hiro tore off his windbreaker and wrapped it around the rope. It would help keep his rope-burned hands from smarting so much. "Go, Jake!" he yelled.

Jake let out a moan and Hiro felt slack on the line. Jake was climbing. Hiro pulled up the slack quickly. "Great, Jake!" he yelled. "Keep coming!" Then he heard a scream of pain, and the rope went tight again. Hiro did his best to take up the slack where the rope was anchored to the pine tree, then looked over the side again. Jake was holding his injured leg.

"Can't climb," he moaned. "Think I broke it, man."

"I'll climb back down again!" Hiro shouted. "Maybe we can rig something up together."

"No. You're probably worn out from climbing down here the first time. Go for help, Hiro. Go for . . ."

Jake seemed to relax suddenly, then go limp. Then rain was coming down steadily. Mud washed against Jake, and down his back.

"Jake!" Now Hiro felt very panicky. He started over the side to climb down the line, then looked down and saw Jake's chest rise and fall. Jake had probably just passed out from the pain, Hiro reasoned.

He stood up and looked toward Portuguese Bend. Lightning or not, he had to get across the open space in a hurry and bring some help. Hiro took off running, but after only a few steps, lightning flashed again, so close that he hurled himself to the ground. He looked around. No more than a hundred yards off, a tree had been hit and split in half. Hiro looked at the pine on the cliff where Jake was hanging. Would it be next? He stood up and coughed away the aching in his lungs. Twisted ankle or not, he had to run. He had to run as hard as he could.

Chapter 5

The rain was really coming down now. Hiro hurried across the huge open area that sloped upward from the cliffs by the sea. He gritted his teeth to fight back the pain of his twisted ankle. There was not so much loose dirt as on the trail to the sea. The ground was covered here and there with grass and weeds, but mostly it was now very muddy. Hiro found his sneakers accumulating mud, his feet getting heavier as he climbed. He stopped to kick the mud off his feet. He was soaked now and cold. As he bent over to push the mud off with a stick, he slipped and fell in the mud.

"Yow!" he yelped. In trying to kick

the mud off, he had forgotten about his hurt ankle. He massaged his ankle tenderly. It was beginning to throb. Hiro got mad again. He refused to let this situation beat him! He growled as he got to his feet, then yelled into the driving rain like a tiger roaring.

Somehow it made him feel better. The ankle stopped bothering him, and his steps were longer. As he made it up the hill and onto the road, lightning struck again, this time hitting a street sign on the road ahead. Hiro glanced nervously back down the hill. He had to hurry or Jake was done for!

The lights were out in the entire neighborhood. Hiro thought of running for help, but decided calling for help was the best idea. Jake would need professionals, maybe people with equipment the people in the neighborhood didn't have. Even if the electricity was out, the phones were probably on. He *hoped*! Anyway, his house was closest.

Hiro hurried toward the back door. Rats! There were no lights on. That meant his mother and father were still out to dinner, talking with his aunt about a business opportunity. What a night to be gone from home.

The back gate was open and banging in the wind. Hiro got inside the fence and shut the gate behind him. But when he got to the back door, it was locked. He reached for his keys, but only grabbed air. The windbreaker! The keys were in his windbreaker!

Hiro looked around frantically. He was losing precious minutes. Summoning all his strength, he backed away a few steps and ran for the door, shoulder lowered like Jake carrying a football. *Bam!* He bounced off the door, onto the back step. Hiro got up and gave it another try, this time roaring like a tiger again. *Bam!* The door burst open!

Hiro grabbed the phone, dialing 911 as soon as he had it in his hand. "911!" he yelled. "Listen, it's an emergency!"

There was no sound. The phones, just like the electricity, were out due to the storm. Hiro sat on a kitchen chair, dripping water and mud onto the floor. Things were looking really bad.

"Think!" he told himself. "What would a real hero do?"

Sure enough, he got an idea. He raced out the kitchen door, leaving it open. The pain in his ankle was forgotten now. Hiro had an idea. He yanked open the side door to the garage and automatically reached for the light switch. When it didn't work, he remembered the big flashlight his dad kept near the door. It worked!

Hiro swept the big beam across the walls of the garage. There against the other side was just what he needed--a large air mattress. Hiro checked the mattress; it was fully blown up and in good shape. Now the other things. He pulled open a door to his dad's tall tool cabinet. There were his dad's sure-grip gloves. Perfect! Hiro put on the gloves and tried carrying the air mattress. It was impossible––the mattress was too wide. He looked around and found some yellow plastic rope. Working quickly, he rolled up the mattress. There! Now he could save Jake!

Hiro fought to get his equipment out of the garage quickly, then headed back toward the cliffs. The rain had let up a little, but it was still coming down hard enough to make it hard to see. As he crossed the road to the cliffs, Hiro forgot to look both ways. *Honnnnkkk*! He jerked around just in time to see headlights bearing down on him. The car whizzed by, spraying water and soaking Hiro even further. But there was no time to bother with it. He hurried down the slope, blinking his eyes. The headlights had blinded him a

little. He stopped, wiping at his eyes, catching his breath. As he looked back up, there was a huge flash in front of him. Lightning hit the pine tree! As he heard the crack of the blast, he jumped to the ground.

Chapter 6

Hiro pulled himself up and looked. It was very hard to see because of the headlights, the lightning, and the rain. He stumbled forward, carrying the mattress. Time seemed to stand still now. He was at the tree in a matter of seconds. He saw that the lightning had hit a tree next to the pine. As he untied the mattress, he saw that Jake's rope was still tight. At least Jake was still there.

Using strength he didn't know he had, Hiro tied the air mattress around his back. Then, using the rope already tied to the tree, he began lowering himself down to Jake.

"Hey, Hiro," came a very weak

voice. "What kept you, man?"

Hiro laughed. Not only was Jake still alive, he could joke at a time like this. But when Hiro got down to his friend, the way he looked terrified him. Jake's face was swollen, his hair matted with mud. He looked awful. Jake was coughing terribly, too.

"I'm cold, man. Really cold."

"I know, Jake. We'll get you out of this."

Hiro secured himself against the cliff wall, digging a couple of footholds out of the mud. He looped his rope around his waist and tied it off. He tested it-- it held. Jake groaned and Hiro wiped mud off Jake's brow. Jake's skin felt terrible, like a cold clam or something. Hiro shuddered, knowing that his buddy was hurt, but kept working.

Hiro got the air mattress ready, then used the same yellow rope to tie the mattress around Jake.

"I got an air mattress," he told Jake.

"I will lower you down to the bottom of the cliffs, okay? The mattress will soften your landing. You'll be all right, okay? Just hold on, Jake. *Please*, man!"

Jake looked at him, his eyes looking hollow from his ordeal. He nodded *yes*, then lowered his head and didn't look back up.

Hiro gazed upward. The rain splattered against the cliff and little bits of mud fell toward his face. He was beyond feeling pain or tiredness. He had never climbed up a rope to the top, but now he had to. He lowered his head, said a little prayer, and started to climb.

The rope was thick and bulky, but the rain had soaked it for a long time now. Still, his Dad's sure-grip gloves helped, and he could make some progress. Hiro looped the rope around one leg as he climbed, keeping himself from slipping back down. He was making it! Halfway up, though, he had to stop and catch his breath. He felt cold, terribly cold all over. He found himself wishing it was all a dream, or some story he made up. That was it. He'd wake up, and Jake would be yelling at him for not timing a climb.

Then another bolt of lightning struck above him. Hiro jerked his head upward and saw a sky lighted up with chains of lightning. Hiro started climbing again, struggling as hard as he could.

How long it was, he didn't know, but it seemed like forever. Still, he was almost there. He could see the knots in the rope where it was tied to the pine tree root at the top.

He needed to reach the top of the cliff, then begin pulling Jake up, out of danger. Did he hear sirens? No, he told himself. He was imagining things. He reached for the tree root, but it was just out of his grasp. Hiro gasped and closed his eyes. He struggled for breath, then pushed against the side of the cliff and made it to the top.

He was across the tree root now. It seemed impossible to get a breath. Hiro felt like a robot, but this robot had batteries that were dead. How he was doing anything, he didn't know, but somehow he fumbled for Jake's rope. Tears began rolling down Hiro's face. The situation was impossible. The only solution was to pull Jake up, instead of trying to ease him down the cliff.

He tied his legs to the tree root, got a grip on Jake's rope, and started pulling. Looking over, he saw that Jake was not moving below. Unconscious, probably.

"More strength!" Hiro yelled at himself. But it wasn't there. He felt his fingers slipping on the rope. And he could feel the rope around his legs coming loose. "Noooo!" Hiro yelled.

"Hiro!"

A pair of strong hands grabbed

Hiro's arms. He felt himself being lifted in space. Was he flying?

He got his eyes open and saw his father holding him. As his dad pulled him back from the cliff, two policemen braced themselves against the pine tree roots and began hauling Jake slowly up the cliff.

"Hiroshi!" his father shouted. "What are you doing, son?"

Hiro could only point below, toward Jake, before he collapsed completely. He could hear his mother crying, coming his way, but he couldn't seem to get his eyes open. It felt like he was slowly falling down a long, dark ditch to someplace where he would finally be safe. *Good*, he thought. *Now if it would only stop raining.*

Chapter 7

Hiro sat up and looked around. There was a television hanging from the wall at the foot of his bed and everything was white. He was in the hospital. He looked to the side of his bed.

"Oh, Hiro!" cried his mother. She put her arms around him. "We were so worried about you! You were so brave!"

Hiro patted his mother on the back, then stopped. His hands were still a little sore. As his mother raised up and dabbed a tissue at her teary eyes, Hiro glanced over at his father.

"What about Jake?" he asked.

His father sighed. "We are not sure.

The doctors say he had much . . ."

"Exposure?"

"Yes, and a broken leg, Hiro. We have prayed for him."

Hiro nodded and leaned back on his bed. All that, he thought, and he didn't even know if Jake would make it. It just didn't seem fair. He looked to the side opposite his parents. He was in a two-bed room, and the other bed was empty. Sometimes, in movies, that meant the other person died, he thought. He closed his eyes and shook his head.

A loud bumping sound opened his eyes. Hiro looked toward the door, and the sight made him sit up again, a big smile on his face.

"Jake!"

Jake grinned. It was a weak grin, but a real one. "Hey, Hiro," he said. "You really *are* a hero. Saved my life."

Hiro was too choked up with emotion to speak. He grinned through

tears at Jake in his wheelchair. There was a big cast around Jake's broken leg. He looked a little water-soaked and weak, but otherwise he seemed fine.

"Thank you, Hiro. Thank you so much!"

HIro looked around in time to see Mrs. Adams give him a hug and a kiss. Mr. Adams grabbed his hand and started shaking it.

"Yessir, son, we really owe ya!"

"Ow!" Hiro yelped. Mr. Adams quickly released Hiro's hand and began apologizing, but Hiro laughed.

"Don't apologize," he said. "I just did what any friend would do. Right, Jake?" But Jake was asleep. Hiro smiled.

"You know," Mr. Adams began, "Jake has been telling me about those stories you write. He's got a little bit of a reading problem, and I was wondering if you could help him improve? I'm willing to pay you for it."

Hiro looked at his father and mother, who smiled. He looked back at Mr. Adams.

"No problem," Hiro said. "But it will have to wait until I finish a new story I want to write."

"About a pirate again?" asked Hiro's mother.

"No, this is a scary story, called. . .'Cliffhanger.'"

Hiro grinned, and everyone began to chuckle.

Artesian Press
High Interest...Easy Reading

Multicultural Read-Alongs

Standing Tall Mystery Series

Mystery chapter books that portray young ethnic Americans as they meet challenges, solve puzzles, and arrive at solutions. By doing the right thing the mystery falls away and they are revealed to have been...Standing Tall!

Set 1	Book	Cassette	CD
Don't Look Now or Ever			
	1-58659-084-7	1-58659-094-4	1-58659-266-1
Ghost Biker	1-58659-082-0	1-58659-092-8	1-58659-265-3
The Haunted Hound	1-58659-085-5	1-58659-095-2	1-58659-267-X
The Howling House	1-58659-083-9	1-58659-093-6	1-58659-269-6
The Twin	1-58659-081-2	1-58659-091-X	1-58659-268-8

Set 2			
As the Eagle Goes	1-58659-086-3	1-58659-096-0	1-58659-270-X
Beyond Glory	1-58659-087-1	1-58659-097-9	1-58659-271-8
Shadow on the Snow	1-58659-088-X	1-58659-098-7	1-58659-272-6
Terror on Tulip Lane	1-58659-089-8	1-58659-099-5	1-58659-273-4
The Vanished One	1-58659-100-2	1-58659-090-1	1-58659-274-2

Set 3			
Back From the Grave	1-58659-101-0	1-58659-106-1	1-58659-345-5
Guilt	1-58659-103-7	1-58659-108-8	1-58659-347-1
Treasure In the Keys	1-58659-102-9	1-58659-107-X	1-58659-346-3
"I Didn't Do It!"	1-58659-104-5	1-58659-109-6	1-58659-348-X
Of Home and Heart	1-58659-105-3	1-58659-110-X	1-58659-349-8

www.artesianpress.com

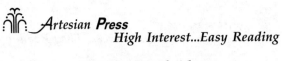

Artesian Press
High Interest...Easy Reading

Fiction Read-Alongs

Take 10 Books

Mystery	Books	Cassette	CD
Nobody Lives in Apartment N-2			
	1-58659-001-4	1-58659-006-5	1-58659-275-0
Return of the Eagle	1-58659-002-2	1-58659-007-3	1-58659-276-9
Touchdown	1-58659-003-0	1-58659-008-1	1-58659-277-7
Stick Like Glue	1-58659-004-9	1-58659-009-x	1-58659-278-5
Freeze Frame	1-58659-005-7	1-58659-010-3	1-58659-279-3
Adventure			
Cliffhanger	1-58659-011-1	1-58659-016-2	1-58659-280-7
The Great UFO Frame-Up			
	1-58659-012-x	1-58659-016-2	1-58659-281-5
Swamp Furies	1-58659-013-8	1-58659-018-9	1-58659-282-3
The Seal Killers	1-58659-014-6	1-58659-019-7	1-58659-283-1
Mean Waters	1-58659-015-4	1-58659-020-0	1-58659-284-x
Sports			
The Phantom Falcon	1-58659-031-6	1-58659-036-7	1-58659-290-4
Half and Half	1-58659-032-4	1-58659-037-5	1-58659-291-2
Knucklehead	1-58659-033-2	1-58659-038-3	1-58659-292-0
The Big Sundae	1-58659-034-0	1-58659-039-0	1-58659-293-9
Match Point	1-58659-035-9	1-58659-040-5	1-58659-294-7
Chillers			
Alien Encounter	1-58659-051-0	1-58659-056-1	1-58659-295-5
Ghost in the Desert	1-58659-052-9	1-58659-057-x	1-58659-296-3
The Huanted Beach House			
	1-58659-053-7	1-58659-058-8	1-58659-297-1
Trapped in the Sixties	1-58659-054-5	1-58659-059-6	1-58659-298-x
The Water Witch	1-58659-055-3	1-58659-060-x	1-58659-299-8
Thrillers			
Bronco Buster	1-58659-041-3	1-58659-046-4	1-58659-325-0
The Climb	1-58659-042-1	1-58659-047-2	1-58659-326-9
Search and Rescue	1-58659-043-x	1-58659-048-0	1-58659-327-7
Timber	1-58659-044-8	1-58659-048-0	1-58659-328-5
Tough Guy	1-58659-045-6	1-58659-050-2	1-58659-329-3
Fantasy			
The Cooler King	1-58659-061-8	1-58659-066-9	1-58659-330-7
Ken and the Samurai	1-58659-062-6	1-58659-067-7	1-58659-331-5
The Rabbit Tattoo	1-58659-063-4	1-58659-068-5	1-58659-332-2
Under the Waterfall	1-58659-064-2	1-58659-069-3	1-58659-333-1
Horror			
The Indian Hills Horror	1-58659-072-3	1-58659-077-4	1-58659-335-8
From the Eye of the Cat	1-58659-071-5	1-58659-076-6	1-58659-336-6
The Oak Tree Horror	1-58659-073-1	1-58659-078-2	1-58659-337-4
Return to Gallows Hill	1-58659-075-8	1-58659-080-4	1-58659-338-2
The Pack	1-58659-074-x	1-58659-079-0	1-58659-339-0
Romance			
Connie's Secret	1-58659-460-5	1-58659-915-1	1-58659-340-4
Crystal's Chance	1-58659-459-1	1-58659-917-8	1-58659-341-2
Bad Luck Boy	1-58659-458-3	1-58659-916-x	1-58659-342-0
A Summer Romance	1-58659-140-1	1-58659-918-6	1-58659-343-9
To Nicole With Love	1-58659-188-6	1-58659-919-4	1-58659-344-7

www.artesianpress.com

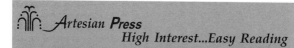

Artesian Press
High Interest...Easy Reading

Other Nonfiction Read-Along

Disasters

- Challenger
- The Kuwaiti Oil Fires
- The Last Flight of 007
- The Mount St. Helens Volcano
- The Nuclear Disaster at Chernobyl

Disaster Display Set (5 each of 5 titles 25 books in all)
80106

Natural Disasters

- Blizzards
- Earthquakes
- Hurricanes and Floods
- Tornadoes
- Wildfires

Disaster Display Set (5 each of 5 titles 25 books in all)
80032

www.artesianpress.com

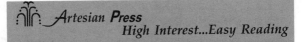

Artesian Press
High Interest...Easy Reading

Other Nonfiction Read-Along

Ancient Egyptian Mystery Series

- The Great Pyramid
- The Lords of Kush
- The Lost King: Ahenaton
- Mummies
- The Rosetta Stone

Ancient Egyptian Mystery Series Display Set (5 each of 5 titles 25 books in all)
80354

Extreme Customs Series

- Body Modification
- Burials
- Fashion
- Food
- Tattoos

Extreme Customs Series Display Set (5 each of 5 titles 25 books in all)
80028